Portia's Prank

Portia's Prank

By

David M. Sargent Jr.

Illustrated by

Jean Lirley Huff

Ozark Publishing, Inc.
P.O. Box 228
Prairie Grove, AR 72753

Library of Congress cataloging-in-publication data

Sargent, David, 1966-

iv

Inspired by

Portia's Prank is inspired by Mary, Vera, Buffy, and Portia. Four little beings who have come into my life and brought with them love, laughter, tears, sometimes a little anger, and even at times, frustration. I know my life is better because of them.

Dedicated to

I'd like to dedicate this book to my parents:
Dave and Sharon Sargent for giving me life;
and
Dave and Pat Sargent for helping me get through it.
Thanks so much. I do love you.

Vera ran screaming to Mary.

"Our ball is missing.
Oh how can this be?
What a sad day for playing,
for we can't climb a tree."

"We'll find our ball," said Mary with force.

"We'll look low and high,
in the fields and the yard,
from the ground to the sky,
though finding it is hard."

Together, they ran yelling to Buffy.

"Have you seen the ball?
It seems to be gone.
There's no fun for all,
until it's come upon."

"Why, no," said the Buff
with no emotion at all.
"I have no idea
where you might find the ball."

Mary asked as they turned to leave,

"If I were a ball,
I would hide where?
Somewhere down the hall?
Maybe under a stair?"

Together they ran looking high and low.

Each place they peered,
there was no ball at all.
Once again they feared
they would never find their ball.

They looked under the bed
and under a chair.
Their hearts filled with dread.
It just wasn't there.

From Buffy there came a holler.
She yelled with fear,
"I saw a prowler!
It was near here!"

Oh, no! they all thought.

And once again they looked
for their toy that was round
in every cranny and nook.
It simply had to be found!

They looked low and high
under sofas and above doors.
They looked toward the sky
and under the rugs on the floor.

Then Buffy remembered
and said with glee,
"Cousin Portia came to visit.
Let's ask her and see."

"Oh, no!" Mary shouted.

"Aunt Mandy just left.
Of Portia there's no sign.
What we have is a theft.
Now, what shall we do with our time?"

They all ran to the bedroom to see a great
sight.

As the covers wiggled
Portia reached for the light.
She said with a giggle,
"Playing with your ball was such a delight.
I'm staying over! Good night!"